THE PIRATE KING

BALISK
THE WATER
SNAKE

With special thanks to Michael Ford

To Adam Ajayi – a hero in the making

www.beastquest.co.uk

ORCHARD BOOKS
338 Euston Road, London NW1 3BH
Orchard Books Australia
Level 17/207 Kent St, Sydney, NSW 2000

A Paperback Original
First published in Great Britain in 2011

Beast Quest is a registered trademark of Beast Quest Limited
Series created by Beast Quest Limited, London

Text © Beast Quest Limited 2011
Cover and inside illustrations by Steve Sims © Beast Quest Limited 2011

A CIP catalogue record for this book is available from
the British Library.

ISBN 978 1 40831 310 7

3 5 7 9 10 8 6 4

Printed and bound by CPI Group (UK) Ltd, Croydon, CR0 4YY

The paper and board used in this paperback are natural recyclable
products made from wood grown in sustainable forests. The
manufacturing processes conform to the environmental regulations of
the country of origin.

Orchard Books is a division of Hachette Children's Books,
an Hachette UK company

www.hachette.co.uk

BALISK
THE WATER
SNAKE

BY ADAM BLADE

ORCHARD

Tremble, warriors of Avantia, for a new enemy stalks your land!

I am Sanpao, the Pirate King of Makai! My ship brings me to your shores to claim an ancient magic more powerful than any you've encountered before. No one can stand in my way, especially not that pathetic boy, Tom, or his friends. Even Aduro cannot help you this time. My pirate band will pillage and burn without mercy, and my Beasts will be more than a match for any hero in Avantia.

Pirates! Batten down the hatches and raise the sails. We come to conquer and destroy!

Sanpao, the Pirate King

PROLOGUE

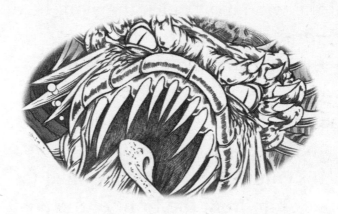

The sun beat down on across Leo's back. The old fisherman let the oars drop from his hands and he stood up. As the sea swell lifted and lowered his little boat, he gazed back to the east. He searched for any sign of the Avantian coast, but the sea stretched all the way to the horizon.

Further out than I've ever been, he thought grimly.

He turned west, squinting into the sun. The air was hot and eerily still;

the sail hung limply from the mast. If the wind didn't pick up soon, he'd be drifting all night.

But that was the least of Leo's worries. He picked up his flask and poured the last few drops of water into his mouth.

His empty catch-basket seemed to mock him from the front of the boat.

"I don't even have a good catch to show for my day's fishing!" he grumbled.

For years the coastal waters had teemed with fish, but in the last few days the shoals had all but vanished.

It's almost as if the fish are hiding from something, he thought with a shiver of fear.

Leo sat down heavily on the rowing bench, ready to take up the oars again in his blistered hands. His

niece, Elenna, would start to worry
if he wasn't back by sunset.

Poor Elenna, he thought as he
rowed. *A girl like that shouldn't be stuck
at home.* Her bow and arrow had
hung on her bedroom wall ever since
she'd returned from her latest
adventures with Tom.

Whoosh! A large wave slapped
against the side of the hull, rocking
the boat. Leo jolted in his seat and
turned.

"A ship!" he mumbled.

A huge vessel carved through the
dark blue waves. She sat high in the
water. Three masts rose from the
deck. The one in the centre seemed
more roughly hewn than the others,
and was slightly bent, almost like the
branch of some huge tree. But the
strangest sight was the blood-red

sails. They billowed, filling with wind, driving the ship onwards. Leo frowned. *But there's no breeze*, he thought.

A single flag trailed and whipped from the odd, central mast. On a black background, it showed what looked like the outline of a Beast's skull, with horns and long, crooked

teeth. *Is it some sort of warship?* Leo wondered. The vessel didn't look like anything in King Hugo's small navy that he had seen before.

Leo waved his arms wildly and shouted, "Over here! Please, help me!"

Even though the ship was still some fifty boat-lengths away, his own craft suddenly lurched. He tripped over, landing on his knees with a cry, and clung to the edge of his vessel. Leo didn't understand – the swell wasn't bad enough to knock him from his feet...

He stared into the water. There was something down there!

A dark shadow, bigger than any shark, drifted beneath the boat with menacing silence.

Leo scrambled to the other side of

his ship, just as the creature broke the surface. He fought the scream that rose in his throat as he saw the snake-like body. Glittering and muscular, the Beast rolled out of the water, sunlight scattering off its silver scales.

Rising up, the monster faced Leo with a head almost as big as his boat. Horns jutted from the head in all directions, and its yellow eyes narrowed to slits. The Beast rose higher still, blocking out the sun. With a hiss, it shot towards Leo.

Leo dived into the water to escape being crushed to death, and heard the crunch as his fishing boat was smashed into splinters. Under the water's surface, he saw the wreckage of his boat sinking. Panic drove the air from his lungs. His heart thudded in terror. The Beast was coming for him, twisting through the water, mouth gaping to reveal deadly fangs. Was this the last thing Leo would ever see?

CHAPTER ONE

A WAITING GAME

Tom threw aside his blanket. He
stared out through the open window
onto a rectangle of night sky.

"It's no use," he whispered.

In the next chamber, he could hear
Uncle Henry snoring softly. Tom had
tried everything – counting through
every Beast he'd ever fought, lying
on his front, on his side, flipping onto

his back. He'd even tried sleeping on the bare floorboards, to remind himself of the many nights spent in the wilderness on his Quests. Nothing worked – he couldn't get to sleep.

"And nothing will work while my mother's lost in a strange land," he muttered.

In some ways, the last Quest in Tavania had been successful. He and Elenna had restored six Beasts to their rightful homes and he'd managed to bring the Evil Wizard Malvel back to Avantia, where he was now imprisoned in King Hugo's dungeon.

It wasn't worth it, Tom thought, his frustration mounting. They'd left his mother, Freya, in Tavania, and Elenna's wolf, Silver – a loyal companion on so many Quests.

How am I supposed to sleep when I've abandoned them?

Tom walked to the window and gazed out. He was sure that Elenna felt the same.

Following their return, the Good Wizard Aduro had told them to go back to their homes – Tom to his aunt and uncle in Errinel, and Elenna to her uncle Leo, a fisherman on the western shore. Aduro had said he'd wanted them both to recuperate after their latest adventures, and that he would do his best to find a way to bring the others home. But Tom couldn't just sit around waiting.

"I have to do something!" he said.

He picked up his shield and sword. He began a series of drills, attacking and backing off from imaginary foes and remembered Beasts: he lunged, thrust and sliced; he ducked, weaved, and leapt; all in determined silence so he wouldn't wake his aunt and uncle.

Soon sweat began to prick across his skin. Maybe if he could tire himself out, he'd at last be able to get some sleep.

Suddenly, the wall in front of him seemed to shimmer, the rough stone melting and blurring. Tom gripped his sword tighter, ready to meet the intruder, and lifted his shield with its six tokens across his body. A shape appeared, vague at first, then growing solid. Tom recognised the floppy cone of Aduro's hat and lowered his shield as the Good Wizard took on his familiar shape.

Aduro peeled away from the wall, and stood in the room with Tom.

Only the slight golden haze
surrounding the wizard's form told
Tom this was only a vision.

"Do you have news of my

mother?" Tom asked immediately.

Aduro shook his head. "You must have patience, Tom."

Tom knew in his heart that the wizard was right, but this did not soothe his restlessness.

"Is there nothing I can do to help?" he asked.

"Not at the moment," said Aduro. "I have sent Taladon in search of something called the Tree of Being. It may have the power to open a portal into Tavania."

Tom's heart lifted. "Where is this Tree?"

"Nobody knows for sure," said Aduro. "Legend tells us that the tree doesn't remain in one place, it's forever moving about our kingdom."

It didn't sound like any tree Tom had ever heard of. "Where is my father now? I'll go with him."

"This is not your Quest, Tom," said Aduro.

"But two warriors are stronger than—"

Aduro raised a hand. "Freya is dear to Taladon, too," he said. "You must let him fight alone."

Before Tom could protest further, the vision of Aduro melted into the stone wall and Tom found himself alone again.

A rustle outside made his skin tingle. He heard the sound of a twig splintering underfoot. Could it be an intruder? Or a fox maybe, after his aunt's chickens?

Tom crept to the window. He heard the snap of a bow-string, then – *whoosh!* An arrow thudded into the wooden window frame.

CHAPTER TWO

TO THE CASTLE

Tom peered out of the window, ready to duck out of sight if the attacker shot again.

Sitting in the crook of a branch on a nearby tree he made out the figure of a girl, silhouetted against the moon. She waved.

Elenna!

Tom ran across his bedroom and pulled open the door with a creak.

He crept barefoot through the kitchen of the cottage and out into the summer night. As he rushed over to the tree, Elenna slipped from the branch and landed, silent as a cat, in the grass. Tom had never been so glad to see his friend. She grinned.

"What are you doing here?" he asked her.

"I can't wait around any longer!" she whispered. "Silver's stuck in another world. Your mother is, too. Every day that passes is a wasted opportunity to rescue them!"

Tom told Elenna about Aduro's visit, and the Tree of Being.

"If it's out there, then Taladon needs our help," said Tom.

A frown passed over Elenna's face. "I agree, but if we can't find this tree—"

"I don't care!" interrupted Tom. "It's my mother we're talking about, and our friend."

"You're right," she said. "Aduro *has* to help us!"

"Wait by the stables," said Tom. He rushed back indoors, more noisily than before, to collect his sword and shield. He was too excited to care about tiptoeing around! As he sat on his bed lacing his boots, Uncle Henry stumbled into the room, rubbing his eyes.

"Is something the matter, Tom? I heard... Are you going somewhere?"

Tom stood up. "I can't say now, Uncle, but you have to trust me. I might be able to help my mother."

Uncle Henry looked worried, but gave a nod. "I understand. Do what you must, but be careful, you hear?"

Tom smiled. "Give my love to Aunt Maria," he said.

He met Elenna at the stables, where she was already saddling Storm. The stallion neighed and tossed his head.

"Looks like he's ready for another Quest," said Tom, as he tightened the straps under Storm's belly. He put a foot in the stirrup and threw himself into the saddle.

"Just the three of us this time," said Elenna.

"Not for long, hopefully," Tom said, reaching down to help her up. "We'll find Silver soon. We have to!"

Storm galloped all the way to King Hugo's castle. The brisk air cleared Tom's head and focused his mind on the challenge facing them: convincing Aduro to let them be

part of this Quest.

They arrived as dawn was painting the sky with pink streaks from the east. The pale stone of the battlements and towers seemed to gleam like gold, and sentries stood guard on top of the walls. Storm's hooves clattered over the open drawbridge and into the central courtyard.

Tom left Storm with a stable-hand. "Take care of him, will you?" he asked.

The boy nodded, and Tom and Elenna raced up the spiral staircase of the turret leading to Aduro's chamber. Tom burst through the door without knocking.

The wizard stood in the centre of the room, his cloak gathered around him. He was uttering a low chant as he stared into a crystal globe. It glowed faintly, and Aduro's hands moved on either side as if controlling some hidden force. So mesmerized with what he was doing that he didn't notice Tom and Elenna.

"Greetings," said Tom.

The Good Wizard jerked his head up and smiled. With a hasty wave of his hand, the glowing orb faded. Tom caught a glimpse of something shimmering in its surface – the shape of a Beast skull.

"Greetings, young ones," said Aduro. "What an unexpected surprise!"

"We want to help," said Elenna. "Has Taladon found the Tree of Being yet?"

A look of anger creased the wizard's face. "I told you, this is not—"

A shout of alarm rose up from the courtyard below. "Fetch a physician! We have an injured man here!"

Tom and Elenna rushed to the window of the turret. A horse stumbled weakly across the centre

of the courtyard, while a groom tried
to grab its bridle. Across the horse's
back lay a man, his body limp and his
hands looped in the reins. The man's
head rested against the horse's mane,

and the back of his tunic was stained red. Tom recognised the chestnut stallion at once, and felt fear clutch his heart.

"Isn't that horse…?" Elenna began.

"Yes," said Tom, his voice cracking with dread. "Fleetfoot."

The blood-splattered man on the horse was Taladon.

CHAPTER THREE

A NEW ENEMY

Tom's blood turned to ice. He ran for the door with Elenna close behind.

"Wait!" called Aduro.

Tom bounded out into the courtyard. A small crowd of stable-hands had gathered, and two of them lowered Taladon from the saddle, turning him over gently.

He can't be dead, thought Tom. "Let me through!"

He gasped when he saw Taladon's face. One eye was swollen shut and his lips were cracked and dry. From a cut on his forehead, fresh blood leaked across his cheek and nose. Tom crouched beside his father, and Taladon moaned softly.

Aduro stood over them, looking on gravely and panting a little after rushing from his chamber.

"What happened?" Tom asked.

Taladon moved his lips, but at first no sound came out.

"Water!" said Tom.

One of the grooms handed down a flask, and Tom tipped a little of the liquid into his father's mouth.

"I found it," he croaked.

"The Tree of Being?" Aduro asked.

Taladon tried to nod. "I came so close, but I was attacked."

"Who did this to you?" asked Tom.

"By…" Taladon's eyes closed.

"Enough questions!" snapped Aduro.

"Father?" Tom said in panic.

Elenna placed two fingers to the side of Taladon's neck. "It's all right. His heart still beats."

"We need to get him to the infirmary," Tom said.

Aduro ordered the grooms to bring a stretcher. As Taladon was lifted up, something dropped from his hand.

"What is it?" asked Elenna.

Tom flattened out the square of rough cloth on the ground. It was dirty white, like sail cloth. In the centre of the square was a symbol he recognised – a Beast skull, staining the cloth red like a bloodstain. Tom looked at Aduro.

"Whose symbol is this?" he asked. "I saw it in the globe in your chamber."

The wizard lowered his eyes and shook his head. "I cannot say."

"Tom, there's something on the other side," said Elenna.

He turned the cloth over. In red lettering, a message was scrawled: *Death has arrived. Yours, Sanpao.*

Tom felt a shudder of dread. "Enough!" he said, standing and facing Aduro. "Why won't you tell us? Who is this Sanpao?"

"He's just a pirate," said Aduro. "No great threat to Avantia."

Tom could hardly believe what the wizard was saying. "No great threat? He almost killed my father!"

"You exaggerate," said Aduro. "Taladon's injuries will soon heal. He will be able to fight once more."

Tom thought he saw a flicker of guilt in the wizard's face. "No!" said Tom, more strongly than he intended. "I will fight this...this Sanpao! The Quest *must* pass to me."

"You mustn't let your anger take over," said Aduro.

Elenna placed a hand on Tom's arm. "Maybe Aduro's right," she said.

"Maybe you should leave this Quest to a more experienced warrior." She winked as she spoke.

Tom could see she wanted him to play along. Something wasn't right with Aduro's behaviour: Tom had never known him to be so unwilling to face up to Avantia's enemies.

"Yes," he said, raising his voice so that everyone could hear. "Perhaps we aren't strong enough for this Quest."

"I'm glad you see sense," said Aduro. He looked to the grooms, then pointed at Taladon. "Take this man to the king's physician, at once."

They obeyed, lifting Taladon on his stretcher. Aduro walked back to his turret. Elenna shrugged at Tom as if to say: *What's going on?*

As the stretcher-bearers passed,

Taladon suddenly came to and reached out with a hand, gripping his son's arm strongly. He raised his body slightly, gritting his teeth.

"Come close," he whispered, his eyes flickering to one side. It was almost as though Taladon didn't want anyone to hear. "Danger lies at sea," Taladon hissed. "Sanpao...he can control Beasts."

Tom's father sank back down again and was carried inside the palace.

"Are you all right?" asked Elenna.

Tom crumpled the sail-cloth in his fist.

"While there's blood in my veins," he said, "I won't rest until Sanpao is defeated. And I don't care if I have Aduro's permission or not."

CHAPTER FOUR

ANOTHER FRIEND LOST

The day had passed slowly, and when nightfall came, Tom and Elenna sneaked out to the stable. The stable-boy was sleeping on some straw, and they crept past him. Storm stayed silent as they fastened the saddle and bridle, then mounted him.

Tom squeezed Storm's flanks and the stallion moved quietly out of the stables and towards the castle gates. The stable-boy jerked awake.

"What—" he mumbled. "No!" He stumbled to stand in front of Storm.

"Let us pass," said Tom.

"But you can't! Strict instructions from Wizard Aduro."

"Tell him we overpowered you," said Tom. "One way or another, we're going through those gates."

He lowered his hand to the hilt of his sword, and the boy's eyes widened. Tom hated using the threat, but there was no time to waste. The boy stepped aside, and Tom kicked Storm into a canter. They surged through the gates.

"Stop!" called a voice.

Tom tugged on Storm's reins, and looked back towards the castle. On the battlements stood Aduro. In one

hand he grasped his staff, and in the other was a torch, trailing flames in the night breeze.

"How dare you disobey me!" he roared. The torch cast orange light over his twisted features.

"We're only trying to help!" shouted Elenna.

Aduro cackled, an evil sound. "You will pay a price for your treachery!" he bellowed.

"We're not the traitors!" Elenna

called back with anger in her voice.

Aduro pointed his staff, and from the tip a blast of purple light spun towards them. Tom didn't have time to lift his shield, and his body shuddered as the magic entered him. When he opened his eyes, he was still seated in Storm's saddle, unharmed. He checked Elenna, but she'd been protected behind him.

"I don't understand," he muttered. "Nothing happ—"

"Your belt!" Elenna gasped.

Tom glanced to his waist. The precious jewelled belt, which held the tokens gathered on his Quests against Malvel's Beasts, had vanished. In its place, a wide sash was fastened around his waist. It looked as if it had been made with some type of animal hide, patchy with mangy fur.

Tom hardly had time to question
what had happened. If Aduro was
their enemy now, the sooner they
put distance between themselves and
him the better. He turned Storm
around again, away from the castle.
Over his shoulder he called back to
Aduro: "Belt or no belt, I won't stand
by while Avantia is threatened!"

"And we won't come back until Sanpao's gone for good!" shouted Elenna.

Tom nudged Storm's flanks and they galloped off into the night.

They headed towards the coast. Taladon's last words were a clue to where to head, and surely any pirates would have to come from the sea. But the Western Ocean was three days' ride away.

"It's a good job we've done so much travelling in Avantia," said Tom. "The quickest way is through the Forest of Fear."

Tom kept Storm at a gallop across the Grassy Plains to the edge of the forest. As the pink of dawn streaked across the sky, Avantia seemed at peace. Tom checked behind them every time they reached high ground, but there was no sign of riders in pursuit. The only person they passed was a woodcutter, leading an empty cart with a nodding donkey.

"What has happened to Aduro?" Tom asked as they trotted into the forest.

"He seems more like Malvel than the Good Wizard of Avantia," said Elenna.

Tom touched the sash, and began to pull it off.

"What do you think that's for?" asked Elenna.

"I don't know, but I don't like it," said Tom, giving up on ripping it off. "It's probably some sort of dirty trick."

Tom felt Elenna grip him a little tighter. "We'll have to be extra careful," she said.

"My father said Sanpao could control Beasts," said Tom. "We need to keep our eyes peeled – they could be lurking anywhere."

"I wish we had Silver with us," said Elenna, peering between the trees. "His nose would be perfect for finding our way."

Tom leant forward in the saddle to hack at overhanging branches. But as the sun rose higher, they met no surprises. The birds sang in the trees and clouds scudded across the blue sky. The kingdom seemed untroubled. Soon the trees began to thin out.

"We're nearing the other side," said Tom.

They passed beyond the wild reaches of the forest to more ordered rows of trees, with small huts and fences. Apples hung from the branches.

"An orchard," Tom said. "We must be near a village." He pulled on Storm's reins, and tensed.

"What is it?" asked Elenna

Tom pointed through the orchard to a tree. A section of trunk had been torn away in the rough shape of a Beast's skull. *Just like the one I saw in Aduro's crystal orb*, thought Tom. Beneath the mark, more bark had been gouged out to spell the message: *Death has arrived.*

"We must be close," whispered Elenna. "Do you think—"

A piercing scream cut her short.

CHAPTER FIVE

A PIRATE RAID

"That way!" hissed Elenna, pointing through the trees. They dismounted Storm and tethered him to a branch.

"He'll be safe here," Tom whispered. A cry of *"help"* drifted through the trees.

With their weapons clutched in their hands, Tom and Elenna darted between the trees into the outskirts of the village as the shouts of alarm grew louder. Tom saw a terrified villager with a cut to his forehead running between two buildings. He sprinted towards him, but Elenna drew him back in the shade of a large wooden apple-press for making juice.

"We can't just rush in," she said. "Let's see what we're facing first."

Tom peered around the press into the village square. Tanned, burly men in heavy leather boots, wearing sleeveless jerkins over muscled torsos, tramped across the square, cutlasses drawn.

"Sanpao's pirates?" asked Elenna.

"They must be," said Tom.

They wore billowing trousers that tapered at the ankles. One passed close and Tom ducked back out of sight. The man wore leather belts around his waist, looped through buckles crafted from polished bone.

"Look at their hair!" whispered Elenna.

Each pirate had the front portion of his head shaved. Some tied their locks in long ponytails that trailed down their backs. Others wore the plait looped around their necks.

Across their bulging forearms, each
had a tattoo of the Beast skull.
Sanpao's mark, Tom thought.

"There are too many to take on,"
Tom said. "We need a distraction."

In the centre of the village square
stood a mighty oak tree. Two pirates,
one on each side, were swinging axes
in turn at the trunk. The leaves
shook with every blow. But why
were they cutting down the tree?

It's no use us storming in, thought
Tom. *Innocent villagers will get hurt.*
He looked around. The apple-press
was a tall wooden structure, on top
of which rested a steel vat. Tom
wondered if he had the strength to
topple it.

The tree in the middle of the square
groaned, leaning dangerously.

"Timber!" The tree leaned to one

side, and with a horrible crunching sound, split at the base. The trunk toppled, crashing through the roof of a cottage and sending a huge cloud of sawdust and leaves into the air.

The pirates gathered around. "So much for magic," one snarled.

"I told you it wasn't the Tree of Being," said the one with an axe, wiping the sweat from his brow. "What a waste of time! We need that tree and its portals if we're to raid the riches of every kingdom we find."

So that's why they are here, Tom thought. *These men are looking for the same thing as us – the Tree of Being. But why?* Tom couldn't believe these tough men were on a quest to help anyone.

"Well, you can tell Sanpao we've failed!" said the pirate's friend.

The man with the axe went pale.

Tom looked at Elenna. "If the pirates get to the tree first, it looks like they'll hack it down," he said.

"And we won't be able to rescue Freya and Silver," Elenna added.

"Help me," said Tom, leaning his weight against the vat. Elenna strained with him, but it hardly budged. Tom dug his heels into the ground and threw his back against the wooden structure. Elenna grimaced beside him, and beads of sweat appeared on her forehead. The vat began to tip. Tom's muscles burned, but he didn't let up until he felt the weight of the vat topple.

"Eh? Look out!" shouted one of the pirates.

Tom almost fell as the vat toppled over. A wave of slippery apple pulp

splashed across the square. The
pirates skidded as they ran away,
losing their footing with cries of
surprise. They landed with a splash,
flailing in the sticky juice of crushed
apple.

Tom and Elenna charged out from their hiding place.

When the tattooed lead pirate saw them, his eyes widened in surprise. He pointed his dripping cutlass.

"Carve them to pieces!" he ordered.

Elenna loosed an arrow, making all the pirates duck. She strung another, and this one buried itself in the thigh of one of Sanpao's men. He screamed in pain.

"They're only children!" shouted the lead pirate.

Tom took a blow to his shield and lashed out, sending the pirate's cutlass spinning from his hand. He kicked another in the gut, who staggered into three others, tumbling them all into the apple pulp.

"Back to the ship!" ordered the lead man, staggering away. "We'll live to fight another day!"

The ship? thought Tom. *But we're still a day's ride from the sea!*

Soon the pirates were fleeing the village. Tom helped up one of the villagers, and Elenna went to check on an old man who had been struck across the cheek.

The villagers gathered around Tom.

"Thank you," gasped the man Tom had helped up. He mopped at his bleeding nose with his sleeve. "Whoever you are, you saved us. Others have not been so fortunate." He shared a nervous glance with the other villagers.

"Go on," urged Tom.

"We've heard these pirates have been wreaking havoc across West Avantia – north of here," he said.

"Then we must go," Tom said.

"Stay on your guard."

The man slapped him on the back. "Good luck, and thank you."

Tom and Elenna walked quickly back to the orchard. He unlooped Storm's reins and caught sight of the tree marking again.

"He won't get away with this," Tom muttered darkly. But at least he and Elenna had been given a glimpse of who their enemy was – the leader of a cruel, ruthless group of men.

Once they were in the open plains again, Tom followed the setting sun westward. The air turned colder with the winds coming off the sea, and he tasted the salt tang on the air. Elenna pointed out that they weren't far from the village where she lived with her Uncle Leo, and suggested they head in that direction.

They crossed the shifting dunes that led to the coast, and soon the silver ocean appeared on the horizon. Elenna pointed to some fisherman's shacks down near the shore. "That's my Uncle Leo's cottage," she said.

They cantered the remaining distance to the shack, and Elenna rushed inside. Tom found her standing in an empty room beside a table. She held a piece of paper.

"What's the matter?" he said.

She frowned. "This is the note I left when I came to find you," she said. "Four days ago!"

"What could it mean?" asked Tom.

"Well, he's either gone away, or..."

"What?"

Elenna turned to him. "Or, he never returned from his fishing trip. My uncle might be lost at sea!"

CHAPTER SIX

THE TREE OF BEING

"Uncle Leo's the only family I've got left," said Elenna.

"Come on," Tom said. "Perhaps the other fishermen know something."

Elenna nodded. Tom could see she was being brave, but he knew all too well that no one could survive adrift in the ocean without water for four days. Outside the shack, two fishermen were tying up their boat to a jetty. Elenna called out to them.

"Have you seen Leo?" she asked.

Both men shook their heads. The older of the two, who had a shaggy white beard and a bald, sunburned head, tipped the basket he was holding to show there was nothing inside.

"Not seen Leo for days now," he said. "There's no fish out there. Maybe he went down the coast, hoping for better luck."

"Why are there no fish?" asked Tom.

The two fishermen shared a furtive glance. "Now don't start that again..." said the younger one.

"Start what?" asked Elenna.

"Father thinks he saw something

out there," said the younger man.

"Something big..." muttered the old man.

Tom looked to Elenna. *A Beast!*

"I tell you one thing for certain," said the older man, "something's not right under the waves."

Dusk set in quickly, turning the sea black. The moon picked out the silver crests of the waves.

"Let's light a fire," Tom suggested.

While Elenna found some oats for Storm, Tom went further up the beach to collect driftwood. The fishermen offered him some dried fish and bread before retiring to their tiny shack. As they sat eating beside the fire, Tom saw Elenna looking out to sea, her eyes shining with tears. He hated to think that Leo had met Sanpao. Or worse, a Beast...

"Don't give up hope," he urged his friend.

"I know," she said. "It's just that I couldn't bear to lose him… Not after—" she paused. "It's late. Let's get some rest. Maybe the morning will bring some more clues."

As Tom lay down beside the fire, he admired his friend's bravery. He tried not to think of his father, lying injured in the palace infirmary. Or his mother, trapped in a foreign land. He drifted into troubled sleep.

Tom woke later with a start, the sweat cooling on his skin. It was still night, but the first hints of dawn washed the sky a blue-grey. The fire had died to just a glow of smouldering orange wood.

"Are you all right?" asked Elenna, stirring.

"I think so," he said. He felt a vibration in the ground, and the embers shifted.

"An earthquake!" he said, springing up.

Storm snorted wildly as fresh flames spluttered then died. The ground lurched and Tom lost his footing, falling in the sand. His eyes fixed on the centre of the fire, where the ground seemed to split apart. With a deep rumble, a spike of bark sprouted, thrusting up and scattering hot coals and sand. It rose, higher and higher like a wooden column, until it towered twenty times taller than a man.

Tom found his voice. "Do you think—" he began.

"It must be," gasped Elenna. "The Tree of Being!"

It was nothing like Tom had
imagined. 'The Tree of Death' would
have been a better way to describe it.
The black bark that covered its trunk
was cracked and diseased, and the

stunted branches had no leaves or buds. Tom circled the tree with Elenna, looking up. The branches drooped, ready to snap. A smell like rotten cabbage filled Tom's nostrils. On one side, where a branch had obviously once been, a round patch leaked sap, weeping like an open wound. There was no sign of any portal.

"If this was once a gateway to another world, I'm not sure it is any more," said Tom.

"Look!" said Elenna, pointing to where he'd been sleeping a moment ago.

There, in the sand, lay his shield. There seemed to be a golden glow around its rim.

"Why's it doing that?" Elenna asked.

Tom picked up the shield carefully, and carried it closer to the trunk. As he did so, it glowed brighter.

"I've always wondered why the shield was so strong," he said. "Maybe the wood came from this tree!"

"Then perhaps it still has some power," said Elenna. "It clearly has a magic connection with your shield. We have to stop Sanpao before he can get near the tree."

"We need a boat," Tom said. "We must meet him head on – out at sea."

He ran across the beach to the fisherman's shack and pounded on the door with his fist. Elenna followed him, leading Storm. The older man opened the door and peered out. "Can we borrow your boat?" Tom asked.

"No point us having it, is there?" said the man, shrugging. "Just bring it back in one piece."

"We'll leave our horse with you as a sign of trust," said Tom. He ruffled Storm's mane. "Don't worry, we'll be back for you soon."

Storm whinnied softly as Elenna climbed into the boat, scrambling over the pile of nets and fishing spears. Tom pushed the little vessel across the sand until they were ankle deep in water, then he hopped on board. Tom and Elenna took an oar each, and began to heave long strokes. The morning sun peeped over the horizon, leaving a golden trail across the Western Ocean.

Elenna, more experienced at sea, hoisted the sail to catch the breeze, whilst Tom scanned the coastline.

If they could get to Sanpao before he even made land, perhaps they could turn them back to where they came from without any bloodshed.

Soon they were cutting through the water by the power of the wind alone. Tom shielded his eyes against the sun, but saw no sign of any life on the waves. Then he spied a shape on the horizon.

"Over there!" he shouted.

Elenna turned excitedly. "Is it my uncle?"

It was a ship – a floating fortress! The craft was huge, with three giant masts and red sails tied with rigging. Spikes jutted from the gunwales and a poop-deck rose at the rear. It stalked towards them through the water, and gradually a familiar shape appeared on its highest flag.

"The Beast Skull!" Tom gasped.
"It's Sanpao's ship."

CHAPTER SEVEN

THE PIRATE KING

The swell from the mighty pirate ship
threatened to capsize them, but Tom
gripped each side to steady himself.
Close up, he saw that the central
mast differed from the other two.
It wasn't smoothly carved and
straight, but twisted slightly in the
middle. Along its length were several
scars where other, smaller branches
had been hacked away. In other

places the branches had sprouted, and were lined with golden leaves.

"It's still alive!" said Elenna.

"That must be the missing branch from the Tree of Being," Tom said, remembering the weeping patch from the tree on the beach. "How could they do such a thing? Does it steal the tree's magic?" He stood up in the rocking boat. "Where's the scoundrel, Sanpao?" he shouted.

The snarling pirates on deck parted, and a huge man stepped forward to the rail of the raised poop-deck. He wore the same sort of clothes as the raiding party Tom had seen in the village, but his garments were all black. The only sign of colour was a sparkle around his waist, hidden mostly in the folds of his clothing. He had a broad chest, and tattoos

climbed up his thick arms. His face
was lined with scars, and his left eye
drooped slightly with an area of pink,
scarred flesh, perhaps from a burn.
His oiled ponytail was studded with
darts.

He drew a curved cutlass from his
scabbard, and held it aloft. Tom
shuddered when he saw the edge

was lined with serrations like shark teeth.

"Did someone ask for Sanpao, the Pirate King?" he bellowed.

"I did!" Tom called back.

Sanpao tipped back his head in deep laughter. "And who might you be, boy?"

"I'm Tom," he shouted. "And you almost killed my father, Taladon."

"I've heard stories about you!" said Sanpao. "Your little friend there must be Elenna."

"His 'little friend' is a match for any of your crew!" she shouted back.

"I guess your nag couldn't join you at sea," continued Sanpao. "And the mutt… Oh, I forgot, he's lost, isn't he? Lost with your dear mother, far, far away!"

Tom's blood boiled.

"How does he know so much about us?" whispered Elenna.

The Pirate King laughed. "I have my sources. By the way, how is my new friend Aduro?"

There was something in the way Sanpao said 'new friend' that made Tom uneasy. Images of the ghostly skull floating in the wizard's crystal ball filled his mind. "Have you done something to him?" Tom asked, snatching up an oar to bring them closer to the pirate ship.

Sanpao's eyes gleamed with triumph. "Aduro grows old," he said. "Weak. Bewitching him was easy!"

"You won't get away with this!" Tom cried.

Sanpao rolled his eyes. "My wizard said you never give up," he said. "If I have to kill you both to get to the Tree of Being, so be it. My Beast is hungry!" He stooped to the deck and straightened up, gripping a conch shell as big as Tom's head. He raised it to his lips, and blew. The noise that came out sounded like a war-horn, and lingered on the still air.

Elenna screamed as a man in rags was shoved forwards between the pirates on deck. "Uncle Leo!"

Two pirates extended a plank over the edge of the ship, and pushed Elenna's uncle onto it. Sanpao strode across the deck and levelled his cutlass towards Leo's throat.

"Time for a final bath, old man."

Leo edged slowly along the plank, which wobbled perilously. Tom felt his stomach sink – Leo was going to be fed to a Beast!

"Don't worry, uncle!" shouted

Elenna. "We'll rescue..."

The words died in her throat as, beneath their craft, the water began to swirl. A shadow moved beneath the waves. For a moment, even the pirates on the deck stopped their jeering. The shadow grew as the Beast surged towards the surface, and Tom pushed Elenna from the side as it burst from the waves. From the sodden boards, he gazed in horror as the Beast rose into the air. The creature's fins were lined with sharp claws and deadly spikes stuck out from its neck. The Beast lashed its scaly, tapered tail into the water, showering them with brine, before crashing into the sea again.

Tom felt Elenna clutch at his arm, and he knew she was thinking the same thing as him. Sanpao's stolen

magic must have been extremely powerful, if he could control Beasts, and use them as his greatest, fiercest servants.

Sanpao pressed the tip of his sword into Leo's back. "Get a move on!" he shouted. "Balisk the Water Snake must be fed!"

Leo's arms flailed, but Tom could see he was going to fall. "Please..." shouted Leo.

Balisk's jaws gaped, revealing needle-like teeth, as it roared with hunger.

CHAPTER EIGHT

A BEAST FROM THE DEEP

"No!" screamed Elenna.

Tom picked up a fishing spear from the boat and hurled it towards Leo with all his strength.

"Grab this!" he shouted.

Leo toppled off the plank as the spear thudded into the side of the pirate vessel. The old man managed to wrap his arms around the shaft,

his legs dangling. The pirates shouted
down curses.

With a roar, Balisk surged out of
the water towards Elenna's uncle.
Leo pulled up his legs with a wail,
and the Beast's jaws snapped shut
a fraction too short.

I have to tackle that monster, Tom
thought, *before someone dies.*

With one foot on the edge of the

fishing boat, Tom launched himself
off. He landed on the Beast's body
just behind the horned head. He
almost slid off the slippery scales,
but managed to hold on to one of the
fins. He gripped Balisk's flanks as if
he was a wild horse. Balisk roared
with fury.

The Beast thrashed in the water,
threatening to tear Tom's arms from

their sockets. Tom managed to draw his sword and struck against Balisk's head with the flat of his blade. He landed a heavy blow, and for a moment the Beast's movements became sluggish.

Through the spray and churning waves, Tom saw that Elenna had sat on the side of the boat and was pulling closer to the pirate ship with both oars. Pirates were hurling daggers at Tom's friend. She ducked aside as the blades thunked into the boat's hull or scythed harmlessly into the water.

"Uncle Leo," she shouted, when she'd positioned the boat below him. "Down here!"

Her uncle let go of the spear and dropped heavily into the fishing boat. Balisk lashed the small hull with his

tail, splintering a plank of wood.
Tom wanted to tackle Sanpao, but
the pirate king would have to wait.

"Fight me!" he shouted at the
Beast.

Balisk stirred beneath Tom,
writhing his muscular body, and
reaching with his snapping snake's
head.

"Drown him!" ordered Sanpao.

Balisk roared and reared higher out
of the water, then plunged beneath
the surface. Tom managed to take
a deep breath as the water streamed
through his clothes and hair. His
knuckles were white where he held
on with all his strength as Balisk
turned over and over, swimming
deeper. The water became colder and
darker, and the pressure in Tom's ears
built until he thought his head might

explode, but still he gripped the fin. He closed his eyes tight and called on the power of Sepron's tooth, the token lodged in his shield. The burning in his lungs stopped at once as the magic worked.

Opening his eyes in the stinging water, he saw the scales the Beast's body weren't the same all over. Along the ridge of his back was a darker strip, the width of Tom's hand, reaching from head to tail.

Balisk twisted violently and Tom lost his grip. As Balisk plunged into the black depths, Tom kicked up towards the surface. He glimpsed the black hull of the pirate vessel to his left. With powerful strokes, he dragged himself above the waves, and sucked in deep breaths of air.

Almost at once, he heard Sanpao

snarl and saw the Pirate King leaning over the edge of the ship. Something glinted in his hand, and he hurled it towards Tom.

Tom dived again, and heard the dart thud into the shield on his back. More darts cut into the water around him. One tore through the shoulder

of his tunic, slicing his skin. Tom gritted his teeth as bubbles escaped his mouth, and a trickle of red blood misted off into the water.

I can't give up now! thought Tom, as he headed for the outline of Elenna's fishing craft. He swam beneath it and came up on the other side. "Give me your hand!" he called.

Elenna leaned over and heaved him into the boat. "Thank goodness!" she said. "I thought Sanpao had hit you!"

Her Uncle Leo was sitting on one of the benches, staring fearfully at Sanpao's ship, which drifted some twenty paces away.

"Coward!" bellowed Sanpao. "Wouldn't it be nice if you could call upon some of your belt's special powers, hero of Avantia?"

With a flourish, Sanpao drew aside his tunic. Tom gasped. Around his waist, the Pirate King wore Tom's jewelled belt! Tom's chest tightened with dismay and anger.

"That belongs to me!" shouted Tom. "I won those jewels through fair combat."

"And I stole them through magic!" sneered Sanpao.

Elenna looked at Tom with desperation in her eyes. "Aduro must have given it to him!" she gasped.

Sanpao dropped his hand to the amber jewel. *He's trying to communicate with a Beast!* Tom realised.

"Men, take arms!" Sanpao roared. "It's time to feed these pathetic Avantians to the fish."

CHAPTER NINE

TWIN ENEMIES

The men shouted their approval and lined up along the deck. Others ran from the stern, holding crossbows made from bone. They aimed their strange weapons. Tom glanced into the water, but couldn't see the Beast.

"While there's grog in my veins," said Sanpao, "you'll never take the Tree of Being from me! Men, shoot!" With a succession of thwacking sounds, the air was filled with bolts.

"Duck!" Tom shouted. He grabbed Elenna and her uncle and pushed them down into the boat as the shafts zipped overhead. The iron tip of one bolt punched right through the fishing boat's hull. But the pirates didn't stop at one volley, and a second hail of bolts shot over the boat. Tom risked a look, and saw that the crossbows automatically reloaded, sliding another shaft into the firing mechanism. Sanpao's laughter cut the air above the whizzing barbs.

"You've not seen weapons like this before, have you?" he called.

Elenna strung an arrow and tried to shoot, but she could only lift her head for a moment before ducking for cover again. "There are too many of them!" she gasped. More bolts slammed into the boat.

"Take us closer, helmsman!" bellowed the Pirate King.

The hail of arrows ceased, and Tom dared to lift his head again. Leo's eyes were wide with fear.

We need help, Tom realised, *before Balisk joins the fight again*. Tom touched the scale embedded in his shield, his link to Sepron the Sea Serpent.

As he did so, spray burst from the water beside the fishing boat, showering them all. For a moment Tom dared to hope that Sepron had come already, but he caught a flash of Balisk's silvered scales. The Water Snake lashed his tail like a whip, driving a wall of water at the boat and sending it spinning on the crest of a wave. Tom and the others gripped the sides to stop themselves being thrown out into the waves.

Elenna managed to string an arrow and pointed it at the Beast. Tom saw her eyes narrow. Suddenly the conch shell sounded again.

The Beast launched itself right out of the water, glowing red for a moment. Elenna shot and her shaft whizzed towards Balisk's head, sinking into the scales in its neck.

"Great shot!" he said.

Sanpao laughed as the Beast hovered in mid-air. Tom gasped as its blunt skull seemed to shift beneath its skin, and its head forked in two. As one half of Balisk crashed into the sea, the other split away along the dark stripe down the middle of its body. This piece, with its own head and fins, soared into the air.

"There's two of them!" shouted
Elenna. The second Balisk used its
fins as wings, propelling it high over
Sanpao's ship.

What are we going to do now? Tom
asked himself.

"Ready arms!" ordered Sanpao.

The pirates rushed around on deck

to load more bolts into their crossbows. Tom realised they were about to face three enemies at once. The bolts locked into place as the Sea Balisk hissed from the water and the Air Balisk began a long swoop towards them. Tom picked up an oar, ready to strike it away.

"Get behind me!" he called to the others.

The pirate ship lurched violently in the water. The pirates toppled into each other and the crossbows clattered to the deck. Two pirates fell with cries into the water. Only Sanpao managed to keep his balance.

"What in the name of the High Seas was that?" he shouted.

A long neck, covered in green scales, unfurled from the waves, cascading drops of water. Sepron's huge, pale eyes flashed with anger, and the sunlight played across the shimmering, rainbow scales.

"Hello, old friend!" Tom yelled.

Sepron opened his mouth and roared back, making the sails on the pirate ship quiver.

"Kill that Beast!" roared Sanpao.

One of the pirates rushed forward with a grappling pole, brandishing it over the deck towards Sepron. The Good Beast closed his jaws, catching the pole and snapping it like a twig.

"Sepron will keep the pirates busy," said Tom. "We need to tackle Balisk."

Elenna was already on her feet, aiming an arrow at the Beast swooping down from the air. Her shaft thudded into one of the horns of its head, making the Beast pull away and hiss with anger. Leo stood

with perfect balance on the edge of
the boat, stabbing with a fishing
spear at the Balisk lurking just
beneath the water. The Sea Beast
darted away, scales glittering in the
sunlight.

Meanwhile, the pirates rushed from
one side of the deck to the other,
looking for where Sepron might next
resurface. Sanpao barked orders, and

none of his attention was on Tom
and his friends.

As the Air Beast darted at them
again, dodging an arrow, Tom threw
his oar aside and drew his sword. In
one smooth motion, he managed to
slice through one of Air Balisk's
horns. The monster hissed in pain,
swooping low across the water above
its swimming twin. Seeing them so
close together gave Tom an idea. If he
was going to defeat Balisk, he needed
them both in one place. *I can't defeat
each of them separately,* he thought. *But
I could conquer them together.*

"I have a plan," he said. "Row us
over to the sea creature."

"Is that a good idea?" asked Leo.

"Trust me," said Tom.

Elenna and her uncle took the oars
and began pulling the vessel towards

the Beast. On the pirate ship, Sanpao's crew pushed the crossbow across the deck to shoot at Sepron.

Tom faced the Balisk that hovered in the sky, the rays of sunlight playing on its scales. Tom raised his sword and pointed it at the Beast. "It's me you want. Let's fight!"

The Air Balisk focused on him with both yellow eyes and roared, angling his body into a dive. Tom saw the sea Beast's dark shadow rippling towards them as well. "Get ready to jump out of the boat," Tom hissed to his companions. "I need to bring the two parts of the Beast back together."

The air Beast opened his jaws, flying down. The Sea Balisk disappeared under the boat as Tom saw his own reflection in the flying Balisk's eyes. Now was the time.

"Jump!" he shouted.

He threw himself off the boat with the others. Turning beneath the surface, he saw the Air Balisk smash through the bottom of the boat and collide with its other half. In a flash of red light, the halves began to fuse together.

Tom pulled himself through the water, sword drawn, towards the thrashing Beast. Balisk faced him as the wings disappeared back into his scaly flesh. The two creatures were morphing back into one Beast.

The Sea Balisk lunged and snapped, but Tom smacked the flat of his blade against its nose. The creature jerked away, turning its back on Tom.

Tom aimed his blade carefully, then lunged and buried it deep in the dark stripe that ran down the Beast's back.

A stream of bubbles exploded from Balisk's mouth and nostrils as it twisted round to face Tom. Though Tom knew the Beast could not speak, through the water the creature's eyes spoke of his pain and confusion.

What have you done? the Beast seemed to say. His eyes shone

brighter than ever for a moment, then Tom watched as the light dimmed and fogged over. The Beast's scales cracked and its body dissolved into the water, leaving only empty ocean.

Balisk was no more.

A single claw from one of the Beast's fins floated within reach. Tom snatched it from the water, and tucked it into his animal-hide sash.

Perhaps this token has some power, he thought. Tom was kicking for the surface, already wondering how he would face Sanpao, when he felt a surge from below. He found himself lifted, dripping, out of the water on Sepron's back. Beside him, Elenna supported her terrified uncle.

On the deck of the pirate ship, Sanpao glared at them with hatred.

CHAPTER TEN

A MAGICAL ESCAPE

Tom raised his sword and levelled the dripping point at the Pirate King.

"Balisk's defeated," Tom shouted. "Release Aduro, and leave Avantia in peace! It's over, Sanpao."

"Over?" Sanpao bellowed. "My voyage has only just begun! Balisk was my first Beast, and my weakest. He's no more precious to me than a ship's rat! There are five more that will prove a stiffer test for you."

Tom felt a surge of pity for the Beast he'd destroyed, cast aside so easily by a cruel man. "While there's blood in my veins, I'll take on every one of your Beasts!" shouted Tom. He looked to Sepron. Tom pointed his sword towards the ship. "You know what to do," he said.

Sepron raised his massive tail from the water, and brought it crashing down. A huge wave slammed against the side of the pirate vessel, throwing the pirates off balance with a chorus of cries. Sanpao held on.

"Sink them!" shouted Leo.

"Is that all you've got?" Sanpao asked. "Helmsman! Take us away!"

"Again!" shouted Tom.

Sepron drove another wave across

the water. It rocked the pirate ship again, but something strange was happening. The vessel seemed to sit higher out of the water than before.

"It's rising!" gasped Elenna.

The water around the base of the hull churned into white foam as the ship rose. More blackened timbers appeared, coated in barnacles. Tom stared open-mouthed.

"Unless your Beast has wings," roared Sanpao, "it's goodbye – for now."

The ship lifted clear of the sea, and water cascaded from the massive hull. Slowly, the ship turned in the air. The wind caught in its billowing sails and Sanpao's vessel climbed away, disappearing to the north and into the clouds. Tom and his companions watched until it was just

a dot near the horizon.

"Sanpao's magic is powerful," said Elenna. "Perhaps he really has bewitched Aduro."

"We should get back on land as quickly as we can," Tom said. "If Sanpao gets there first, he'll hack the tree down."

"We've lost the oars from my boat," said Leo. "What will we do?"

Sepron hissed and turned her head to look at them.

"I think we might have some help," said Tom, smiling.

"I've never travelled so fast!" said Leo, gripping the edge of the fishing boat. "It's like a water chariot!"

Tom and Elenna grinned as the spray soaked their faces. A rope trailed from one of Sepron's fins to the prow of the boat as they shot through the water towards the coast. When they reached the shore, Sepron released them. The boat drifted the rest of the way to land.

Tom, Elenna and Leo jumped out and tugged the boat in, wading up to their ankles in water.

"Thanks, Sepron!" shouted Tom.

The Sea Serpent lashed the water with his tail and gave a roar of farewell. Tom's heart swelled with pride as his Beast friend's shimmering coils sank beneath the waves.

They'd landed some way up the beach from where they'd left Storm, so Tom and Elenna ran along the sand near the water's edge. The stallion whinnied happily to see them. Beyond him, the Tree of Being cast a long shadow across the beach. There was no sign of the pirate vessel. As they walked closer, Tom realised the Tree had changed since the last time they'd been here.

"The trunk looks thicker," he said, stroking the bark. Even the branches seemed more healthy.

"Perhaps it's because we defeated Balisk," said Elenna.

She must be right, Tom thought. Seeing life return to the mighty Tree filled him with hope.

"Maybe when we've vanquished all of Sanpao's Beasts, the Tree will be completely healed," Tom said. "Then the portal might appear to help us rescue my mother and Silver."

"I hope so," said his friend.

The ground shuddered violently beneath their feet. Tom and Elenna

gripped each other and Storm reared
up, neighing in panic.

"What's happening?" Elenna
shouted. The sands shifted around
the base of the trunk, collapsing
away to reveal the tree's gnarled
roots. With a sound of cracking
wood, the stunted branches folded
down against the tree's trunk, then
the central pillar began to sink into
the ground. Tom remembered what
Aduro had said about the tree
moving from place to place.

"It's disappearing!" he gasped.

As the knotted tip of the tree
vanished from sight, the sand
reformed over the top. Tom walked
over. Something was left in the sand.

Tom crouched down and found
what looked like a scroll.

"It's bark!" he said, unrolling the

rough parchment.

Elenna stooped at his side. Shapes
had been etched onto the surface of
the bark, leaving different shades of
brown colouring. The reliefs depicted
a sketch of the entire Avantian
kingdom. It wasn't as detailed as
some of the maps Tom had used, but
he could feel the powerful magic
through his fingertips.

"Look, Tom," said Elenna, pointing
to a spot in the Grassy Plains. The
small shape of a tree had been
scorched into the bark.

"The map must tell us where the Tree will next appear," said Tom.

"But Sanpao might by flying there already," said Elenna.

Tom curled the map up and slotted it into Storm's saddle bag. "No time to lose then." If Tom had any chance of seeing his mother again, he'd have to defeat his most determined and double-crossing enemies yet. *Sanpao is my enemy*, he thought. *And Aduro?* Tom felt sure he was under the Pirate King's thrall. There was nothing for it – no one could save Freya and Silver except Tom and Elenna. They had to return the Tree of Being to full health.

"This isn't going to be easy, is it?" Elenna asked, as they climbed into Storm's saddle.

"Do you want to turn back?" Tom

asked her. He felt a sharp pinch on his back and cried out.

"I came to get you! Remember that girl in the tree? I never turn back."

Tom nodded as he pressed his knees into Storm's sides and the stallion trotted along the beach. "I know," he smiled. "I was just testing."

Elenna waved to her Uncle Leo, who was walking towards them.

"Off so soon?" he shouted. "Perhaps I can give you some dinner?"

"Sorry, Uncle," said Elenna. "Sanpao won't stop. Neither can we."

Her uncle nodded and smiled. "Take care of her, Tom," he said.

Tom grinned. "It's Elenna who looks after me," he said, giving Storm's flanks a nudge. *We'll need each other more than ever this time,* he thought.

Join Tom on the next stage
of the Beast Quest when he meets

KoroN
JAWS OF DEATH

Win an exclusive
Beast Quest T-shirt and goody bag!

Tom has battled many fearsome Beasts and we want to know which one is your favourite! Send us a drawing or painting of your favourite Beast and tell us in 30 words why you think it's the best.

Each month we will select **three** winners to receive a Beast Quest T-shirt and goody bag!

Send your entry on a postcard to
BEAST QUEST COMPETITION
Orchard Books, 338 Euston Road, London NW1 3BH.

Australian readers should email:
childrens.books@hachette.com.au

New Zealand readers should write to:
Beast Quest Competition, PO Box 3255, Shortland St,
Auckland 1140, NZ or email: childrensbooks@hachette.co.nz

**Don't forget to include your name and address.
Only one entry per child.**

Good luck!

All books priced at £4.99,
special bumper editions
priced at £5.99.

Orchard Books are available from all good bookshops, or can
be ordered from our website: www.orchardbooks.co.uk,
or telephone 01235 827702, or fax 01235 8227703.

Series 8: THE PIRATE KING
COLLECT THEM ALL!

Sanpao the Pirate King wants to steal the sacred Tree of Being. Can Tom scupper his plans?

978 1 40831 310 7

KORON
JAW OF DEATH

978 1 40831 311 4

HECTON
THE BODY SNATCHER

978 1 40831 312 1

TORNO
THE HURRICANE DRAGON

978 1 40831 313 8

KRONUS
THE CLAWED MENACE

978 1 40831 314 5

BLOODBOAR
THE BURIED DOOM

978 1 40831 315 2

Series 9: THE WARLOCK'S STAFF OUT NOW!

Malvel is up to his evil tricks again! The fate of all the lands is in Tom's hands...

978 1 40831 316 9

978 1 40831 317 6

978 1 40831 318 3

978 1 40831 319 0

978 1 40831 320 6

978 1 40831 321 3

The Chronicles of Avantia

FROM THE DARK, A HERO ARISES...

Dare to enter the kingdom of Avantia.

A new evil arises in Avantia. Lord Derthsin has ordered his armies into the four corners of Avantia. If the four Beasts of Avantia can find their Chosen Riders they might have the strength to challenge Derthsin. But if they fail, the land of Avantia will be lost forever...

FIRST HERO, CHASING EVIL, CALL TO WAR, FIRE AND FURY OUT NOW!

www.chroniclesofavantia.com